PURR-FECTLY WISE

Kimberly Palmucci

Illustrated by Brandi McCann

One warm, bright morning,
on a day much like today,
Wise Kitten woke to the sunlight,
his fur a light shade of gray.

1

Unlike the other kittens he knew,
at play with their sisters and brothers,
Wise Kitten always wanted to learn,
ask questions, find answers, help others!

2

Wise Kitten was born without a home;
on the streets he would walk and wonder,
"Is there a place where I can feel safe
from rain and the big boom of thunder?"

3

One day, as Wise Kitten hid from a storm,
beneath a forgotten blue car,
a wise passerby saw him hiding alone—
"You poor thing—look how frightened you are!"

The man scooped him up, dried off his fur, and with a hug, their bond was written. He knew even before they went to the vet that he'd never part ways with Wise Kitten.

The years went by; the kitten grew,
observing life, studying this, learning that.
And before the Wise Man knew it,
Wise Kitten became a very Wise Cat.

The pair spent their days together,
best friends, loyal and true.
Each sunrise brought new adventures,
as their bond to each other grew.

Wise Cat's life was bright with fun,
toys, treats, and love without end.
But one day, Wise Cat noticed
a slowdown in his trusty old friend.

Both knew that their time together
was a gift that could never be measured.
With gratitude and sadness,
their last moments together were treasured.

Wise Cat was taken to a shelter,
feeling sad and empty, as anyone would.
How he missed his friend who had saved him—
recalling good times as much as he could.

He thought of the words of the Wise Man:
"In great sadness, there can also be light."
He vowed to be kind, spread his wisdom,
and honor their friendship so bright.

11

So Wise Cat woke the next day
to a warm uplifting sunrise.
A three-legged cat in the cage to his right
was resting with despair in his eyes.

Sensing sadness in his new neighbor,
Wise Cat decided to reach out.
Wise Man would want him to help, be kind—
give advice to a soul filled with doubt.

Helping another through hard times,
he knew, would have made Wise Man proud.
He vowed to keep sharing his wisdom,
which helped clear his own dark storm cloud.

As days swept by like autumn leaves,
with each day bringing new light,
a young woman opened the door to his cage,
allowing new hope to take flight.

She looked in his cage, and into his eyes,
"You have much to offer this world, yet!
You're wonderful, kind, and patient—
my home needs a wise, senior pet!"

"Your eyes show you have lived a long life
with memories of days more carefree.
But you have so much living to do still—
would you like to make more, with me?"

As Wise Cat left his cage that day,
he realized a new chapter had begun.
He cherished the memories of Wise Man,
but his days of happiness were not done.

18

He'd spent so much time telling others
they were perfect, strong, and brave,
he'd forgotten his end was important, too—
senior pets are vital to save!

he curled into his warm cozy bed,
f to dream of fun places to roam,
sighed and knew Wise Man would be happy
at his Wise Kitten had found a new home.

The End

Made in the USA
Middletown, DE
11 March 2019